PLEASURES OF CRIME 4

by

David Chaloner

A CIP catalogue record is available for this title from the British Library

ISBN: 9798396735187

Cover image: *Chop Suey* 1929 by Edward Hopper. Collection of Mr and Mrs Barney A. Ebsworth.

Chapter 1

Amy looked moodily out of the upper floor window of her apartment on Pacific Heights. It was a cold January night and unusually for San Francisco frost sparkled on the sidewalks and windshields of cars in the light of the occasional street lamp. Arctic weather gripped North America. In Chicago it was minus forty Celsius.

And the Underwood case still *gripped* her. (See *Pleasures of Crime 3*.) Eddie and April had told her to forget it, these things happened, you had to move on. Never take it personally.

But she did take it personally. She had seen through Carole Underwood, seen through her right from the start, seen through her seductive games, her vacuous intelligence, her low cunning.

She sipped her bourbon on the rocks, the ice melting, smoked her way too expensive Dunhill cigarette – she couldn't stand American cigarettes. She never felt more English than when she thought of bitches like Carole. It was partly her absurd snobbery, what was it Carole had said to Eddie? Fourth generation San Franciscan? She and her husband Horace – Horace! -in league with that

3

murderous cunt Ethel thought they could amuse themselves not only by leading the cops up the garden path but the top California PIs too! Well, they hadn't fooled her, Amy Fairfax. No sir.

Another woman might have taken solace from the fact that she *had* understood Carole, instinctively understood her, but Amy knew from her earliest years in convent school in Liverpool that there were *never* any excuses. Amy's religious beliefs had evaporated at least a year before she had first been fucked by Johnny Reid at the age of fifteen, though contradictorily she still experienced visitations by the Devil at climactic seizures, most effectively so. But the Catholic discipline, that was something she understood; that, though she never admitted it, was the source of her superiority, her authentic superiority.

And it was that unspoken, that unthought of intimation that burned her up. Amy kept her fundamental arrogance discreetly hidden. If April or Eddie ever had gotten a sniff of it they would have rationalized it as her Englishness which would have only demonstrated their fundamental American ignorance of the English.

So Amy suffered, as they had been taught to all those years ago, knowing that any further investigation of Ethel and the Underwoods was strictly verboten. Verboten by

Eddie but by something else as well. Obedience. The most powerful word in the English language.

Chapter 2

In the meantime there was the matter of the missing fifteen year old girl. Her parents – both successful architects – lived at the top end of Hyde Street. Elsie – Elspeth – had been missing for over a week. The police had been informed but hadn't seemed to have made much progress. Plus there were a lot of fifteen year old girls who went missing. It was what fifteen year old girls did. Most of them returned after dad or mom closed down their credit or debit accounts or they got bored with their hot eighteen year old new boyfriend.

Amy met the parents at the practice offices they headed as partners in the business district just off Montgomery. They hadn't wanted to meet at Hyde Street because of the younger children and the nanny, they were sure that Amy understood. Amy agreed reluctantly – a visit to a fifteen year old's bedroom was often revealing.

Even after a minute it was obvious how angry the father was and how much he blamed his wife who sat tight lipped as he asserted how over indulged the girl had been. He had tried repeatedly, over and over again, to point out the inevitable consequences of giving a fifteen year old Elsie a free rein at Magnin's or whatever had replaced it or promised her a Beemer for her sixteenth birthday coming up.

That was not fair, Alan, the wife who was called Susan not Sue had riposted. Elsie had worked hard at her single sex private school, was a high achiever. Just like you said Alan sarcastically.

Amy gently explained that it would be enormously helpful if they could suggest any possible reason for the girl's disappearance.

"Nothing, complete fucking mystery!"

Amy looked at his wife.

"I don't know." She hesitated. "There might have been a boy."

Alan exploded.

"Boy, what boy? First I've heard of any boy. Now you tell me!"

Susan had had enough.

"For fuck's sake, Alan. She wasn't about to tell you because she knew how you'd react …"

"How old is the *boy*, I mean are we talking statutory rape, are we talking some criminal thirty year old fucking rapist, is that why I know nothing about this *boy* …?

"I rest my case," announced Susan and sat silent in her chair.

Outside there was the continuous murmur of conversation from the draughtsmen's offices that Amy had passed through en route to the Cromwell's private room.

Amy tried again.

"Do we know anything about this young man? His name, is he in high school for example, have you met him?"

"Apparently, Elsie and a couple of friends from school went dancing at this … disco, or whatever they call them now, and met these boys …"

"Jesus!"

"For Chrissakes, that's what girls and boys do, they meet! They meet in cafés and dance places and they meet and kiss and neck. What were you doing when you were sixteen or did you magically miss out on adolescence and suddenly jump from twelve to thirty five?"

"I've had enough of this shit, I'm going to call the police. This puts a completely different complexion on things."

And left the room.

"He can't stand not being in control. Do you want a drink? I'm going to have one."

She strode over to a cupboard and found a bottle of Jim Beam, glasses and bottled water. She poured out two large measures, poured water into one of the glasses and lifted an eyebrow as she held the water bottle over the other. Amy nodded and Susan added a splash of water. She handed the glass to Amy.

"Cheers."

"Cheers."

"I don't know much about him, the boy I mean. I do know Elsie liked him very much, she said he was real nice and treated her well. I didn't get the impression necessarily that his parents were well off or that he went to a private school. I got the feeling that he was just a nice boy."

"When did she tell you this?"

"Not quite a month ago. They used to meet after school apparently."

"With her girl friends.?"

"I don't know. Maybe."

"It would be helpful if I could meet some of her school friends."

"Janet Suarez and Chrissie Middleton were her closest friends. I think the police have spoken to them and their parents."

Amy put their details into her iPhone.

"Do we need to sign any documentation?"

"No, all that has been taken care of when you dealt with Eddie. We have all rights to pursue our investigations as is appropriate. Both you and your husband are our clients. I'll follow up these girls."

"Thank you for being so patient. Alan gets super anxious where Elsie is concerned."

She found her own way out.

Chapter 3

Eddie and April sat smoking their cigarettes in Eddie's office. April rarely smoked. Outside large snow flakes slowly drifted down.

"Coffee?"

April nodded.

He pushed the intercom button.

"Two coffees, Julia."

Eddie sighed.

"Have you heard from Amy re the missing girl?"

"She's met the parents. Apparently Dad is an asshole. Went bananas when Mom revealed there was a boyfriend. He started talking about statutory rape."

"He was probably worried."

"Is that the first thing you think of when you hear your daughter has a boyfriend?"

"A daughter who has gone missing for over a week!"

Julia put two coffees on Eddie's desk. Left.

"Whatever. At least it gives Amy something to do. She was wound up tight."

"She's got to learn to let go."

April blew out smoke.

"She's convinced the Underwoods collaborated with Ethel Rivers to murder her husband. Five will get you ten she's right!"

"That's not how it works. All we have is one fat theory. There're a million theories in our business."
April stubbed out her Lucky.

"How's Kirsty?"

"Good, I think."

"Have you mentioned the idea that she might join us?"

"I'm not sure that business can justify another investigator at the moment, plus there's the problem of space."

"We've got two desks in my office. There's plenty of space for a third. And we're turning away work. Did you take on the Cromwell case to give Amy something to do?"

"Partly," Eddie confessed

"You can't baby her. She's got to grow up sometime. She's over thirty now."

"Amy will be fine. You shouldn't underestimate her. She's got good instincts."

"That can go with being a tad neurotic!"
Eddie gave her a hard look.

"Amy has faced pressure before. Remember the Russians."

"She's not the same as us, maybe it's the English bit and she's got that …"

"That what?"

She stood up.

"Forget it. I have to do some shopping at Macy's. I'll see you later."

He watched her beautiful ass twitch as she went through the door. The Underwood case was still getting to them he thought.

Chapter 4

He threw Molly against the wall. Her head connected sickeningly. Dazed, she slid down her black high heels scrabbling against the carpet. He threw her over the back of the chesterfield, pulled aside the string of her G and pushed his beaked fingers into her anus. Pushed. She gasped. Pushed. Half his hand in her rectum. Reached down. Slapped the side of her face with his free hand. Felt the pleasure of his cock hardening. Pushed. Hand full in. Female swearing. Moving his hand. Felt a turd with the tips of his fingers. Turning of his hand. Female gasping. Female groaning. And more groaning.

"You bastard."

"Dirty cunt."

"U-U-U-H."

Female come.

He pulled his hand out and thrust in. Ten thrusts and it was his turn.

"U-U-U-H."

Sexual intercourse Eddie J style. He pulled the beautiful girl off the black chesterfield, slapped her again and told her to make some coffee. She staggered off in her torn G-string and black high heels.

He slumped into the chesterfield. He thanked god for Molly. The slut was the only thing that kept him sane. He did not know what he would do without her. He loved the big heavy buttocks of Sandra and her Mom, loved to fuck his three bitches, April, Amy and Kirsty, all such smart girls. But Molly was different, Molly was his thing.

When he had met her Molly was arrogant. She knew she was a red headed beauty with a perfect white body. With high perfect tits and a matching neat butt, men and more than a few women lusted after her. Eddie puzzled her, he expressed little interest and she slowly realized that this indifference had begun to excite her. But what excited her most of all was first his contempt for her – as she experienced it – and then his assertion that she was just a sexual object that he would do what he wanted with. What excited her particularly was that he made no attempt to please her or care for her. He fulfilled her rape fantasies and more, but it was his contempt that she needed above everything. Such a perception of some women's needs was once commonplace; everybody knew there were some females who needed rough sex to come. Strangely, de Sade was blind to this fact mainly because he was almost entirely focused on male sexual satisfaction, torturing women – and children – was his main interest, despite

Juliette he had little interest in female pleasure. Many a man has been surprised when a women is juicier after a beating or even if he takes her arm roughly. So if it might seem a little self serving for Eddie to understand that he gave Molly what she needed actually he was right. After *Fifty Shades* we know many women like a good spanking or more to come but for Molly it went further. She needed to be violently tortured. There are people like that male or female.

Sipping their coffee he looked at Molly's crafty smile and felt the weight of the Underwood case slip – if only temporarily – from his shoulders.

"Bitch!" he smiled.

Chapter 5

April had a weakness. She liked to be fucked by killers. One in particular. His name was Juan Cortez and he lived in one of the painted ladies, colorfully painted Victorian houses on Alamo Square, north east of the Haight area. His own painted lady was a seventeen year old slut who was there to service his and his guests' wishes. April had last seen him at a private orgy on Balboa that was noteworthy for being conducted in complete silence except for the sounds of the thrashing of limbs as beautiful girls were strangled to death and the concomitant grunts of pleasure as men and women fucked. April's cunt leaked as she remembered being fucked by a line of men. (See *Pleasures of Crime 2*.) She was known to him under the alias of Susie, a whore who also worked in the darker end of the porn business. She called him now.

"Hello."

"Hi, baby, guess who!"

"I've no idea, identify yourself."

"It's Sexy Susie, baby. Hot from Hollywood.

"Hi. What were you doing in the big H as if I didn't know."

"They're getting dirtier. Imagine me walking along Sunset in my hot tiny dress, no panties, at dawn after a night of fucking and all these derelicts grab me and gang rape me, strangle me as they do so and leave me lying naked on the sidewalk, presumably dead."

"Sounds good to me. Let's have dinner tonight."

"The Carnelian Room at eight. Know it?"

"I'll be there."

The last time she had been at the Carnelian was when she had eaten there with Denis Matthews presently languishing on death row at San Q guilty of second degree murder though pleading that after collaborating with the cops availed him nothing. Her finest hour she thought, getting him to confess ie boast on video with sound. Cortez had been at the same party but knew nothing of her PI work. For Cortez she was just another of his several dirty sluts, the only kind that were any good to him.

She wore the black tight skirt suit that Deirdre, dressmaker to many of the high end West coast whores, had made for her. It was cut low at the front barely restraining her large – natural! – breasts and tight over her ass – tighter now that she had put on a couple of pounds. She knew it turned Juan on.

She felt the silence as she strutted in to the Carnelian Room. Without looking she knew all the people were staring at her. They all knew that she was a whore.

Juan dressed in his usual black double breasted suit with the faint blue chalkstripe didn't stand as she arrived. You don't stand for prostitutes. It turned April on being treated like a slut. As in.

"Hello, slut."

"Hello, Juan."

Throughout the meal he verbally abused her. Asked how her tits felt how her cunt felt, was her asshole lubed. She answered him in kind as she cut her delicious steak, drank the wonderful red burgundy which she knew cost over $200 a bottle.

They didn't talk as he drove her to Alamo Square in his black Ferrari. Inside his house he pulled up her skirt and fucked her lubed asshole as his house cunt pulled down her bodice and sucked and bit her big tits. Later she shat on the girl's face as Juan fucked the teenager's anus, pulled out and fucked April's shitty ass again. So it went on for at least an hour. They finished by taking turns to thrash the naked slut with a long bamboo cane. It was only when she saw blood streaming that April finally relaxed and began to get over the Underwoods and a thousand other things.

Chapter 6

Chrissie Middleton sipped her flat white and looked warily at Amy.

"You're British."

"I grew up in Liverpool but I'm naturalized."

Chrissie nodded. She had untidy straw colored hair, blue eyes and slight acne. She wore an expensive pink cashmere sweater and cargo pants. She looked like what she was a rich, slim girl of fifteen or sixteen. Her parents had wanted to be in on the interview but Chrissie had brusquely asserted. No way.

"What kind of girl was Elsie?"

Chrissie took another sip. Shrugged.

"Just an ordinary girl. She's nice. A good friend. A fun person."

"Have you known each other a long time?"

"Sure."

"How long … approximately."

"Couple years. We arrived at Larch House the same year."

"Larch House – that's your school?"

"Yeah."

"Apparently there's a boy involved."

"What do you mean involved?"

"Elsie was seeing a boy."

Another sip.

"We were all seeing boys it was no big deal."

Chrissie cleared her throat.

"And you met these boys how?"

"Different ways, different places."

"Cafés, discos?"

Chrissie grinned.

"Discos, right!"

"But there was no particular boy ..."

"Particular ...you mean special?"

"Yuh."

Another grin.

"There were a lot of special guys!"

"How old were these guys?"

"Not old. We weren't about to be creeped out!"

"Eighteen, nineteen, twenty? Older?"

"Whatever. Sure."

Amy felt like screaming.

"Do you know where Elsie is, Chrissie?"

A blink. One blink from those baby blues.

"If I knew we wouldn't be having this conversation."

"Why not Chrissie?"

"Because I would have told the cops and everybody else!"

"Would you, Chrissie?"

"Yes, and stop calling me Chrissie. My name's Christine."

The girl was staring at her furiously.

"You know where she is, no, let me rephrase that, you have a very good idea where she is!"

"I want to go now."

"Sure, you're free to go."

The girl got up and left. Amy sipped her cold espresso. She wondered if Janet Suarez would prove to be any more forthcoming.

Chapter 7

Janet Suarez was a Tex Mex sixteen year old beauty. Long black hair, oval face, dark brown eyes, light brown complexion, red lipstick on a full mouth to go with the deep red micro dress that showed off long shapely legs and a neat butt down below and pretty tits above. Her red high heels were Manolo. She was fragrant in a freshly showered kind of a way. She had the kind of looks that would slow the traffic right down as she strode along the sidewalk. Amy later found out that her father was a big wheel in big pharma down in Houston and their house in the Presidio was just one of several they had in Texas and the West Coast. She spoke in the soft slow tones that all beautiful women affect knowing that everyone male or female is hanging on her every word.

Yes, she knew Elsie well. A pretty girl, very popular, no? Also a very smart girl. Smart at school? Of course, but also smart in life. She knew not to waste her time with some people. What kind of people, Janet? She tossed her long black hair. You know – people you cannot connect with. She spoke softly and adorably. The type of people you know are losers. Amy nodded as if she understood. So Elsie liked winners?

Janet shrugged, sipped her coffee. Of course.

Amy moved in.

"And this boy she was seeing, did you know him?"

"What boy is that, Amy?"

"The special one, the one she was in love with."

"Ah, there were many boys in love with Elsie. She was sexy, no?"

"Was she, I didn't know that."

This sixteen year old going on thirty was beginning to get on Amy's tits, as they say in Liverpool.

"Si, she could fuck all night long, two or three boys. Two Es to stay awake and she would fuck. Two boys at the same time. Look, I have a picture of Elsie holding two cocks on my phone."

"Could I see?"

"Sure. I help your investigation, no problem."

She fished out her iPhone flicked through the apps and showed a picture of a pretty naked dark haired girl sitting between two boys of sixteen or so, an erect cock in each of her small hands.

Amy took out her own iPhone. She knew the girl had her number.

"Sure."

Amy saw the pic on her phone.

"Any others?"

"An ass shot, I think. Si. You want?"

"Yes, please."

Close up of white ass cheeks pulled open by the same small hands. A smiling Elsie looking over her shoulder at the unseen photographer. Presumably one of the boys.

"She wasn't shy!"

"She had a nice ass. She told me she liked anal. Everybody does anal."

Amy nodded.

"Do you know these boys?"

"These boys? No, they are not my type. Too young for me. I like men."

Amy could see that.

"Do you know where Elsie is, Janet?"

"Nobody knows. She has disappeared. Disparut. Gone."

"Thank you, Janet."

"De nada. Nothing."

Chapter 8

"Is this Elsie?"

Amy held her iPhone with the cropped face of Elsie Cromwell up to the well-groomed face of Andrea Lennox, principal of Larch House School. She was a dark haired woman in her fifties dressed well in a brown tweed skirt suit and light brown court shoes. Under it she wore a white blouse and a discreet pearl necklace.

"Yes, that's Elsie."

Amy had explained earlier that she was a licensed investigative agent working for Jackson and Major International here in San Francisco hired by Elsie's parents to investigate the disappearance of their daughter.

"We were wondering if you could throw any light on Elsie's disappearance. Was there anything in her recent or past behavior that might offer any clues?"

Andrea Lennox clasped her hands together on the leather framed blotting pad on her rather beautiful light walnut desk. Amy felt it was a characteristic radiating respectability and trustworthiness.

"I wish I could offer something helpful. Elsie was a hardworking student of above average intelligence. She was open, friendly and direct in her dealings and exhibited

27

few if any signs of anxiety. She had several friends and her school reports were generally positive."

"There were no disciplinary problems?"

"None."

Ms Lennox's eyes were green and frank and confident.

"I have spoken to Janet Suarez and Chrissie Middleton. Apparently they were her close friends?"

"I could confirm that."

There was the faintest tightening of the Lennox mouth.

"Any comments on these two young ladies?"

"Like Elsie they were both A grade students. Smart, hard working girls, friendly and direct. Very much typical Larch House … young ladies to use your words."

Amy smiled.

"Well, it looks like a complete mystery from your point of view!"

"And from yours too it would seem?"

"'fraid so. Was there anything, anything at all, Ms Lennox?"

"If there was I would have told you so. We're all at Larch House extremely concerned for Elsie."

"If I hear anything perhaps I could come back to you, ma'am?"

Andrea smiled graciously.

"Of course."

"Thank you."

Both women stood and Amy walked out the door. Her thoughts as she left circled around the revelation that everybody was lying to her.

Chapter 9

Amy had been reading from her notes. When she had finished she put the dossier on Eddie's desk. For security reasons reports were never communicated on line. Outside on Post Street faint traffic noises made their way into the office. The winter sky was a brilliant blue but it was still cold. Very cold.

"It's not much to go on," said Eddie.

"Chrissie Middleton knows where she is, or at least has a very good idea and if she does the Suarez girl knows too. She's just better at hiding it."

"What about the parents?"

"I'd say their blaming of each other was genuine. Very bitter. Mom was holding stuff back from dad but I don't think she knows the identity of any notional boyfriend."

"Is there a boyfriend?"

"Mrs Cromwell said Elsie talked about one. He may or may not know anything assuming he exists. We know Elsie is pretty wild from the two pricks pic."

"I wouldn't make too much of that, Amy, kids send these sexy pics to each other all the time!"

April leant forward and picked a cigarette out of the office silver box. Lit it with the office Ronson. She glanced at Amy who was studiously looking at her lap.

"But the parents don't know about these sexy pics."

"Of course not, Eddie!"

April smiled and looked tolerantly at her boss.

"And what about the school principal?"

Amy's eyes flashed as she answered.

"She's a bitch, she knows something!"

There was an awkward silence. April opened her mouth and closed it again. The Underwood case still haunted them all (see *Pleasures of Crime 3.*).

Eddie nodded.

"Anything else?"

Amy was defiant.

"Something about this case stinks. There're too many people lying!"

Eddie was silent for a beat. Then.

"OK. I suggest we surveil the two girls. Fortunately, it's a day school. They've met Amy so that will be your job, April. Amy, try to connect with one of the staff members at the school without tipping off what's her name Lennox."

Amy had calmed down.

"OK, boss."

"That's it," said Eddie and the two women left. Eddie sipped his cold coffee. Looked out the window at the blue sky. Picked a cigarette out of the box.

Chapter 10

Larch House was a large mock Tudor building abutting the Presidio set back some significant distance from the West Pacific Road. There were indeed a couple of larches but also a cypress and one or two redwoods. Somewhere a woodpecker was hammering away and a jay flashed blue among the trees. There was a lot of green grass emerging from the melting snow. A bright golden sun was heading west. April sighed happily and lit her second Lucky of the day. There was no sign that it was a girls' school. She looked at her Jaeger-LeCoultre. Nearly five o'clock. As if by magic expensive automobiles began to park along the side of the road. April heard a bell ringing some place.

Girls of every age between eleven and eighteen began to walk, run and dance out of the main entrance. They were dressed in every kind of casual wear but even from this distance through the trees that shaded the layby in which she had parked her black BMW April could see that this clothing was universally clean, decorous and expensive. Their hair in every possible kind of style was shining, neat and empty of any kind of artificial color. If they wore make up it was barely noticeable and their faces were smiling, shining and bright. It was a picture from a more innocent and long gone age. In the chatting exuberant crowd she recognized Chrissie Middleton and Janet Suarez striding purposefully together. They got into the back seats of a well preserved classic light green Pontiac driven by a blond haired boy of around twenty. April spied a darkhaired youth in the front passenger seat.

The Pontiac jumped off with the roar of a tuned V8. April gave it five seconds and smoothly followed. It was a fairly empty road at this time of day and April kept her distance. Driving fast was a smart thing to do if you were concerned about being surveiled and April allowed herself to be overtaken by another car full of girls and parents.

The Pontiac cruised fast downtown on California finally stopping outside a Starbucks on Fillmore. The quartet got out of the car and sauntered into the café. April parked a little distance away and followed them in. The two girls and the boys sat together in a booth by a window. April sat at a small table close to a middle aged man who was reading a Chronicle and took no notice of April as she sat down and ordered a latte. The body of the man reading his paper shielded April from the direct sight of the four young people.

They spoke loudly and enthusiastically mostly about the shortcomings of other girls or teachers. They used words

34

like "gross" and "insane" and "really stupid" and nudged each other and spilt their coffee and generally behaved like teenagers do all over the States. The boys acted cool, laid back, making a soft male obbligato to the female descant arpeggios. April sipped her coffee and listened to the routine assertions of the American teenager. There was absolutely nothing to catch her attention. And then.

"Plus we've had all these questions about Elsie. The school, the cops – even a private detective woman. She was weird. English. Imagine an English private investigator."

It was Chrissie speaking.

"Did she have nice tits?" One of the boys.

"Aw, Steve, it's always tits with you. Don't you ever think of anything else?"

"Sure, sometimes I think of asses. Nice juicy asses!"

Scuffling and giggling. One of the boys – the blond guy – turned round and shouted at the Puerto Rican waiter.

"More coffees all round. Same as before."

"So what gives with Elsie?" The dark haired boy. Janet's soft, seductive voice.

"No one knows. She's disappeared. Gone."

"Gone where?"

"Nobody knows."

"Sure, somebody knows."

"Really, Steve, nobody knows."

"Somebody always knows. That's the rule."

Steve had gone up a notch in April's estimation.

"Who was that loser she was hanging with. I bet he knows something."

Janet's soft voice.

"He says he knows nothing, Johnnie."

"I bet he's lying. He's a real weirdo. And he lives south of Mission. What a creep!"

"Sure you're not jealous, Johnnie. I thought you were pretty keen on Elsie!"

"Bullshit, she's not my type.

"Tits not big enough?"

"Cut it out, Chrissie."

It was a cold command and the little group fell silent. After a while there was some desultory conversation which ended when the girls asked Steve to drive them back to their respective homes. Steve left a $50 bill on the table and they all mooched out. Their good mood seemed to have evaporated. April let them go and ordered another latte.

Chapter 11

When April had gotten back to Post Street she filled in Amy regarding the conversation she had overheard.

"Chrissie accused her pal Johnnie of having a crush on Elsie. Johnnie didn't like that."

"What do we know about Johnnie?"

"Dark haired guy about twenty. Uptight compared with his friend Steve, same age, blond and confident."

"Thanks, I'll call Janet."

Amy's fingers danced over her iPhone.

"Janet? It's Amy from Jackson and Major. That's right. We're interested in your friend Johnnie. OK, he's not your friend. Just give me his details. Johnnie Collins. Trainee accountant. Address and cell number. OK. And while I'm about it same for Steve. Never mind how I know their names. Just give me his details. Steve Bradshaw. And his details. OK, thanks. And Janet … it's very important that this conversation is confidential, tell no-one and I mean no-one. Elsie's safety is paramount. Do not compromise her life. Yes, it's that serious. Thanks, Janet."

"Can you trust her?"

Amy shook her head.

"Nowadays I pretty much trust nobody!"

April nodded.

"Who are you going to contact first?"

"Johnnie. I'll do it now."

She called him. He answered immediately.

"Hi, my name's Amy Fairfax, I'm with Jackson and Major, Private Investigators here in San Francisco. We're investigating the disappearance of Elsie Cromwell who I believe you know."

"You're the English female detective."

"I'm naturalized. We would like to meet with you as soon as possible."

"What happens if I don't want to meet with you?"

"I call the authorities and tell them we have grounds for thinking that you may be involved in Elsie's disappearance. It's me or the cops, buddy."

Silence. Then.

"There's a place on Geary downtown. The Jackdaw. Know it?"

"Yeah, I know it."

"I'll see you in an hour at twelve. You're paying."

He rang off.

April raised an eyebrow. Amy smiled.

"A real charmer! I'm meeting him at the Jackdaw at twelve."

"He's dark haired, lean … and tricky!"

"Thanks!"

Chapter 12

She didn't like him. He was a goodlooking kid with even features, hazel eyes, thick dark brown hair, lean and tall but broad shouldered, he was any sixteen year old female's dreamboat but Amy didn't like him. After one hostile stare he avoided her gaze. He didn't offer to shake hands and she got the impression that he rarely smiled.

"Hi, I'm Amy Fairfax. I'm a licensed investigator at Jackson and Major Investigators here in San Francisco. We're investigating the disappearance of Elspeth Cromwell. OK, first off, is there anything you'd like to eat?"

"Ham, cheese and relish sandwich on rye and a Coors beer."

Amy signaled for the waitress and gave the order.

"Twice."

"Yes, ma'am."

"What kind of person was Elsie?"

Johnnie shifted in his seat.

"Just an ordinary girl. Nothing special."

"Smart? Attractive?"

"Sure."

"Did you fancy her?"

Those cold eyes flicked over her face, her body.

"Fancy?"

"Did you like her sexually?"

Hostility blazed momentarily in those hazel eyes.

The waitress arrived with their beers and sandwiches.

"Thanks," said Amy.

"You're welcome."

"Isn't that kind of personal?"

"Answer the question, please."

"No, I didn't fancy her. She wasn't my type."

"What is your type, Johnnie?"

He didn't hesitate.

"Someone more like you. A grownup woman who knows what she wants."

Touché.

"So why are you and Steve hanging out with these under age chicks?"

One shrug. And began to eat his sandwich. Took a sip of the beer.

"I understand Elsie had a boyfriend."

Another brief, unfriendly glance.

"I understand you thought he was a little déclassé, that he was a bit out of her league."

"He was a creep."

41

"How so?"

"He was just a silly little kid."

"Does he have a name?"

"Billy something. Billy Martinez."

"What did he do?"

"He did nothing. He was a high school senior. A loser."

"That's a little unfair, isn't it?"

Another shrug. More eating of sandwich. Amy started in to eating hers. It was good. She drank some Coors.

"I still don't get why you hang with these schoolgirls."

He looked at her cynically.

"Sure you do."

She let that pass.

"I understand you're training as an accountant. What's your aim in life, Johnnie?"

"Make money!"

"That's it, make money?"

"Make money and have fun!"

She looked at him steadily.

"Hardly original."

"Fucking's not original either. People still like to do it."

"So you like fucking?"

For the first time a smooth smile.

"Don't you?"

"So who are you fucking at the moment, Johnnie?"

He didn't like that.

"Fuck you."

She nodded.

"Did you fuck Elsie?"

He stood up abruptly.

"None of your fucking business."

"I'll take that as a yes then."

He walked out. She ordered a coffee.

Chapter 13

She met with Billy Martinez in a coffee house off Union Square. She had gotten his cell number off of Janet Suarez. He was a nice looking boy of seventeen or so. The last time he had seen Elsie was two or three weeks back. He didn't know she was missing. Amy stared at him.

"You must be the only friend of hers that doesn't know that!"

He looked at her steadily.

"I had no idea. She was fine when I last saw her."

"Which was where?"

"We used to meet at this diner on Mission. It was kind of our special place."

"So this would be after she left school in the afternoon?

"Check."

"So this would be after she had returned to school after the Christmas vacation?"

"Right."

"Early to mid January?"

Billy nodded. That was around the time Elsie had disappeared.

"Can you remember what you talked about?"

"Just the usual stuff. She studied modern literature, I mean that was one of her favorite subjects. We had our favorite authors. Wolfe, Fitzgerald, Kerouac."

Amy smiled.

"American Romanticism!"

His face came to life.

"That's so cool. But you're English, ain't you? Do the English know about American writers?"

"You'd be surprised. The only English Romantic writer is D H Lawrence so …"

"Lowry, Durrell?"

She felt her eyes opening. Wow, this kid was bright. He was still talking.

Have you read *Under the Volcano*?"

She nodded.

"That's so cool. We must get together with Elsie!"

"Elsie's gone remember. Did she not say anything? Anything at all?"

"No."

For the first time he looked upset.

"This isn't some kind of joke?"

"No, Billy. Her parents are desperately worried. So are Janet and Chrissie."

"Janet's all right. I never cared for Chrissie."

"And her parents?"

"I never met them. I think Elsie had issues, especially her dad."

"Do you know what kind of issues?"

"Elsie said that he was a bully, never listened."

"Elsie was young, a lot of young people have issues with their folks."

"I know. I had the feeling this was different."

"What kind of different?"

"She clammed up when I pressed her. She was closer to her mother, I think."

Suddenly, he looked bewildered. He might be knowledgeable about the modern novel but he was still a seventeen year old boy just out of childhood.

"Billy, you've been very helpful. Here's my card, if you can think of anything that might be relevant, just call me, OK?"

He looked stunned.

"I will see Elsie again? She's ... she's really important. Please find her."

She saw the tears in his eyes. She touched his arm briefly.

"Try not to worry. These things usually work out."

She left him very alone staring at her almost imploringly.

Well, Elsie had at least one person who really cared. She found the Lexus where she had parked it and drove back to Post Street. There was something about this case that was starting to get to her.

Chapter 14

Midnight Saturday night found Eddie and April being entertained at Jimmy's, Bulgarian Georgi's lapdancing club. Eddie and Georgi were sitting together on a sky blue leather chesterfield looking through the huge plate smoked glass window at the scene below in what was unofficially called the Gang Bang room. Maria, the black German slut was kneeling between Eddie's thighs fellating him just as a blonde teenager was doing the same for Georgi.

In the vast room below them April was the centerpiece. Dressed in black transparent bra and panties, black garter belt, black sheer stockings and shiny black high heels she leant comfortably against another leather chesterfield – black. The tiny bra barely restrained her large tits and the lacy thong only emphasized her large protuberant ass which shook slightly as she shifted on her heels, smoking a cigarette.

She was surrounded by a large crowd of heavily built men all naked which revealed many tattoos on often hairy bodies. These were men who did not share the modern young urban males' obsession with smooth shaved skin. They were after all mostly gangsters. Scattered among them were young universally beautiful women dressed generally as April was. Microphones picked up their calm and generally quiet insults directed at April; slut, whore and dirty bitch being the most printable. As she heard the words, Maria licked the tip of his glans with expert subtlety. She was known for her oral skills.

Georgi grunted with satisfaction as the contemptuous words reverberated around the observation room. His blonde bitch bit gently on the hard tool in her warm mouth.

April sighed with relief as she heard the expletives, threw down her cigarette and stubbed it out with the sole of one vertiginous heel, her tits and ass shaking slightly as she did so. The hand that had been holding the cigarette slipped to the black nylon covered cunt and gently stroked her clit. Almost immediately she squirted on to the floor and at this signal, the crowd moved in slapping and biting and inserting cocks and hands into her anus, cunt and mouth. There were flashes as men and women captured the moments on their cell phones or filmed the action, to be found later on various porn sites.

Incredibly excited April climaxed incessantly as cocks and hands stretched her cunt and asshole. Within minutes she was covered in sperm, piss and shit as countless men and females relieved themselves on her beautiful, albeit scratched and bruised body. Some of the most vicious blows came from gorgeous women, faces distorted by hate, who scratched and bit her tits and buttocks.

Eddie now buggering his black bitch could barely see April's blonde hair as she lay on the ground trodden by heavy feet as gangsters and their sluts ejaculated, pissed or squatted over her. The more vicious attacks were interrupted by Georgi's bodyguards scattered among the orgiastic throng.

After nearly an hour of this onslaught, men and women drifted away to find their clothes and drink heavily while four men lifted April's limp and filthy body on to the chesterfield and gave her a large whiskey to revive her. Eddie relaxed as Maria jerked his cock and came over her insolent face.

Later, April showered, scented and dressed in her black whore skirt suit joined Eddie and Georgi in the bar to relax with Georgi's Four Roses bourbon.

Chapter 15

Amy was sitting opposite a pretty dark haired woman in her late twenties in a secluded table at the Villa Capri. It was the first time Amy had visited since the gunfight there nearly two years ago. (See *Pleasures of Crime 2*.) The young woman's name was Julie Sacks and she was Elsie's literature teacher at Larch House. Once again Janet Suarez had been helpful. Their tagliatelle starters had just arrived. Amy was dressed somberly in navy sweater and blue Levis. Julie sported a woolen lumberjack shirt and tight green cord pants. Dark blue sneakers. They sipped the delicious Chianti.

"This is a lovely place. There're so few authentically Italian restaurants in San Francisco now."

"We love it especially since it's so close to our offices."

"How come an Englishwoman is working in a PI outfit in America?"
Amy smiled sweetly.

"It's a long story. I used to work in television in London. A lot of that was investigative work. It seemed a natural progression."

Amy thought it wise not to allude to the Russian gangsters who had driven her to seek sanctuary with Eddie. The two women concentrated on the wonderful tagliatelle. Julie put down her fork.

"How can I help you?"

"We understand that Elsie Cromwell was very interested in modern American and English literature, especially the novel. Could you corroborate that?"
Julie took another sip of wine.

"She was super keen. She was a passionate reader and very insightful about every aspect of writing, character, style, context. She is only nearly sixteen but I would say that her understanding was way beyond her years."

"And she was communicative about her interests – with you, with her classmates?"

"Very much so. She was quite assertive, actually very assertive and I would say dominant in class discussion. She was particularly interested in Kerouac, I recall."

"On the Road!"

"On the Road, Big Sur – all the classics."

"Do you think that Kerouac wild individualism fed into her life?

Julie hesitated.

"Possibly to some extent. She and her friends went out with older boys who were into things like hot rodding not a million miles from Kerouac, I guess. But a lot of girls in their mid teens go for that life style – and to a degree talk about it with their teachers. As you know the hormones go a little crazy at that age girls and boys both.

"How did she get along with her parents?"

"She didn't talk about her folks a lot. That's completely normal at that age. They're into believing that they're now grown up. I got the impression that she was closer to her mother than her father. She occasionally spoke about projects her mother was involved with. Both her parents work as, run an architectural partnership. Successfully so, I believe."

"So you can throw no light on her disappearance?"

"Girls occasionally do run off for lots of different reasons. Conflict at home, running off with a boy – or girl sometimes. It's a dramatic age. But here's the thing. I was not entirely surprised."

They were interrupted by the arrival of their main courses. Amy continued.

"Go on."

"I said that Elsie was communicative and confident. But there was something else as well."

Amy stared.

"It's difficult to put my finger on it. I felt the overt confidence was a bit of a front. There was also something guarded, even secretive about her personality. I don't know how many people would have been aware of it."

"You're the first person to mention it."

"It was so fleeting. I … I was reminded … do you know that Keats poem *Lamia*?"

"Sure."

"Today it's regarded as a little misogynistic reflecting Keats's anxiety about women, though there's little sign of it in *Eve of St Agnes*, wonderful sensuality but …"

"*Lamia*."

"There's that look the doomed young man briefly sees in her eyes."

"The look of the serpent – like in the Garden of Eden, the fatal Eve, yeah, that's pretty misogynistic!"

"Now you're making me feel bad. Maybe you should forget I said anything. It's so easy to imagine …"

"No Julie, that's very helpful. Sometimes that's all we have to go on. Some little thing, but you pull on that little thing and the whole mystery unravels. Can you remember the context of this look?"

"No, I can't. It's just something that happened that one time."

There was nothing else of note that emerged from the conversation. Julie was a little subdued for the rest of the meal as if she had revealed something that perhaps she shouldn't have. Amy knew about that. She remembered her last case, remembered Carole Underwood, she knew all about individuals who kept their mysteries hidden behind a confident exterior. You saw something through the mist and then it was gone and you wondered if you had imagined it. Yes, Amy knew all about that.

Chapter 16

It was over two weeks and nobody had heard anything. The police had spent time with Alan and Susan Cromwell, with Andrea Lennox and with Chrissie and Janet. April, still satisfyingly bruised under her sweater and jeans had followed Johnnie Collins, was following Steve Bradshaw. Johnnie worked downtown in a large accountancy firm, still lived with his parents in the Richmond area of Western San Francisco and had little social life.

Steve was a different case entirely. He worked in a large insurance company Campbell Assurance on Montgomery Street, had his own apartment in the Haight area, drove a souped up Pontiac as noted and seemed to hang with a lot of goodlooking babes in their early twenties, late teens and a fewer number of male friends of his own age. April followed him around in her BMW, keeping her distance and making sure she wasn't recognized. He occasionally got together with Johnnie and he spent a little time with Janet Suarez who seemed to unbend a little in his presence. She actually deigned to laugh at what April observing from a distance assumed were his jokes. As a goodlooking twenty year old he was playing the field. April, however,

56

in her cynical fashion wondered if he were just too good to be true.

Her presentiment was reinforced by one peculiar feature of his otherwise blameless life. Steve liked whores. And not just the usual call girls. There was an upmarket brothel in the Mission district that he frequented. April knew it. She had visited it with Juan Cortez on more than one occasion.

It was a large, comfortably furnished Victorian house, decorated in the style of that period. It specialized in under age girls, mostly fifteen to seventeen who dressed in schoolgirl gym outfits without panties or tartan microskirts with white cotton knickers. Japanese style Hello Kitty colorful clothes also had their followings. These girls wandered around the various rooms lit by twinkling chandeliers and in this cold winter roaring woodfires. Middle aged men and a few of their wives and mistresses would grab girls and fuck them almost always brutally.

April, dressed in suitably sluttish style, followed Steve in one time and saw a different Steve. As soon as he had entered he grabbed the first girl to hand, threw her over the back of a large armchair and buggered her savagely. April licking another girl's little tits watched from a few feet away. He left her weeping real or fake tears and strode out of the house. April let him go, concentrating on the clit and holes of her girl. She needed to relax and take in what she had just seen.

Steve's actions had opened up a completely new dimension. It was as if she had entered another universe. She shouldn't have been surprised, it was a world that April knew very well. She had gone to many brutal orgies in the Bay area, she knew the true nature of Man. She thought of the naked Elsie that Amy had shown her, Elsie holding the two erect pricks of the naked boys on each side of her. Elsie would have fitted in just fine in that big, warm house.

Chapter 17

"So what do we know?"

Eddie was at his most urbane in his Harris tweed jacket, striped Brooks Brothers shirt, Ralph Lauren tie and Loake brown suede brogues. (His trip to London a few years back had not been entirely wasted. See *The Golden Key*.)

Amy explained that she had now interviewed Elsie's mysterious boyfriend one Billy Martinez. He was a high school senior about seventeen, smart, interested in modern literature both American and British. Had known nothing about Elsie's disappearance and was consequently upset and worried. Amy discounted him from any involvement in the affair. She had also spoken with Johnnie Collins. She saw him as arrogant, aggressive, probably insecure and still living with his parents. Almost certainly hung up on Elsie though denying it. Claims to know nothing about Elsie's vanishing. Could be telling the truth. Finally, had spoken at some length with Elsie's English teacher at Larch House. Confirmed Elsie as smart and mature beyond her years, apparently confident and dominant in classroom situations but something secretive and disturbing at least to her.

"Name?"

"Julie Sacks, spelt as it sounds."

"April?"

"Trailed Collins, lives at home as Amy says. Got nothing. Steve Bradshaw is something else. Blond haired stud, drives classic hot Pontiac, popular, sexy babes love him, plus star struck male cronies like Collins. Which is why it's unusual he visits the Chicken House …"

"Chicken House?"

"Upmarket brothel in the Mission area. Specializes in under age girls. Constantly visited by the cops who have almost certainly been paid off. No doubt the cops get freebies."

"Thanks," said Amy. "Helps explain why he hangs out with Elsie and the other schoolgirls."

"Any sign that Elsie or the other girls are connected to the brothel?"

"Not so far, Eddie."

April crossed her legs. She was still turned on from watching Steve fuck his girlie over the back of the sofa. Eddie repressed a smile. He knew April from way back.

"Well, it seems to be warming up. April follow the brothel angle. Amy what about the two schoolgirls. Chrissie Middleton and Janet Suarez. Do they know anything?"

"Chrissie's nervous, she might. Janet's way more sophisticated. She's not going to do anything that would compromise her family in Texas. She'd take the long view. A cool customer."

"And the parents?"

April picked a Lucky out of the silver box.

"I'll have a shot at Dad. That anger could be hiding something."

"Go for it. And Amy try Middleton again."

"OK, boss."

And that was pretty much that.

Chapter 18

Yet she knew she had made no real progress. All the young people she had spoken to were just that, ordinary young people. Chrissie rebellious and resentful, Janet cool, beautiful and calculating, Johnnie a likely mommy's boy, somehow jealous and embittered, jealous of Steve; Steve arrogant, charming but more than slightly vicious. They all had the potential to be criminal but so did fifty percent of rich American youth. Most of them would go on to become middlingly successful professional Americans like Alan and Susan Cromwell.

Amy fretted in her Pacific Heights apartment. She thought of her own youth in Liverpool, her reasonably successful career in television, her own need for danger and sexual abuse that led to the excitement she derived from hanging with Russian gangsters in London, meeting Eddie who had saved her bacon and given her a new life. Any one of these young kids could be another person like her, another Amy looking for thrills and frustrated with the conventional middle class world. She wondered what would happen to Billy, idealistic intelligent still innocent Billy. Life was tough for the Billys of this world; he might settle for becoming a teacher like Julie, perhaps with a derivative typescript in a drawer someplace, his homage to Fitzgerald or Hemingway.

God, she was in a terrible mood tonight. She lit one of her English Dunhill cigarettes and poured herself a bourbon and water. Amy had yet to learn that private investigation work is mostly wasted work. That breakthroughs come rarely and in some cases not at all. In most occupations you do some work and you have something to show for it. Private investigation work is mostly the intellectual equivalent of beating your head against a wall. Nothing in Amy's previous life had prepared her for nullity. That was why the Underwood case had hit her so hard. It was the first time that failure had slapped her in the face. And it looked like the Cromwell case was more of the same.

Chapter 19

Around noon April spent half an hour at the Chicken House. She explained she was on a missing person case and showed the motherly proprietress pictures of Elsie, Chrissie and Janet on her iPhone. The woman shook her head. No, she had never seen them. April thanked her left her card and vamoosed. She wasn't sure that the woman didn't recognize her from one of her occasional visits with Juan Cortez. If she did she made no sign of it. In any case this was a woman who was used to keeping the secrets of her clients.

She surveiled Alan Cromwell over the subsequent days. When he wasn't in his practice he was out entertaining clients sometimes with his wife, sometimes without. Away from his wife he was jovial and goodhumored, smiling and talkative. With his wife Susan he seemed guarded allowing her to do most of the talking. There was little sign of the fury that Amy had reported and April wondered if the younger woman had once again been exaggerating as April thought she characteristically did. Seeing the couple together April got the impression that it was Susan who was the confident one. She knew from experience that male architects were often on the autistic spectrum, suffered from dyslexia and not infrequently were borderline psychopaths. Alan she thought could be any of these.

Plus he was pretty well behaved. She saw him when he was alone with staff or clients on numerous occasions and though as we have noted he was capable of charm he was not overtly flirtatious.

She arranged for a young whore she knew to make a pass at him when he was eating alone in a restaurant on one of those rare occasions when he was alone. The girl was very attractive, a graduate of Stanford where she had studied fine arts, wondering if she could join Alan at his table as it was so crowded and she had persuaded the maitre d' that she was his guest, would he mind terribly? Alan had smiled and acquiesced and they were soon talking animatedly as April watched from a distance. Later, she discovered that predictably they had talked about modern Californian art and sculpture but that Alan had not risen to the bait of having a drink with the girl in her hotel room. What was wrong with the man April had thought exasperatedly as the gorgeous creature finally strode off. Was he in the closet? A lot of designers were gay. Or this guy was super disciplined. Again, April was sophisticated enough to know that the one thing that all architects had to be was disciplined. All that architectural drawing. Or despite all appearances from Amy he was actually devoted to his wife?

April returned home to her house on Pacific Heights in a thoroughly bad mood. She thought of calling Eddie and asserting that the guy was squeaky clean. Experience held her back. Never be fooled by appearances.

Chapter 20

Chrissie Middleton didn't want to meet with her again. Amy had been pretty insulting frankly, had all but called her a liar. After Janet, Elsie had been her best friend. Amy noted the past tense, but didn't pick her up on it instead she apologized, admitted she had been trying to provoke Chrissie, she had been clumsy, apologized again. Everybody was really upset about Elsie's disappearance, her parents especially. Plus it was only a matter of time before the police released pictures of Elsie to the media. There was a pause. Amy pressed her iPhone to her ear.

"I guess it would do no harm to get together if you think it might help."

"I appreciate that, Chrissie. Shall we meet at the same place off Union Square? I'm in the area, could you get off school for a couple of hours, I'm sure they'll be understanding."

Another long pause.

"Chrissie?"

"I'll see you there at noon, if there's a problem I'll call you."

Amy exhaled. She hadn't realized how tense she was.

On the dot of twelve Chrissie came into the coffee house. This time she was wearing a demure floral shirtwaister and white sneakers. She was grinning, pleased to be out of school.

"I said I was feeling sick!"

Amy smiled.

"That would be understandable given your circumstances."

She looked blank for a moment and then nodded.

"That's true. People have been pretty understanding."

"I think it takes a while for these things to sink in. It must be very upsetting for you. The fact that your friend, your close friend just completely disappeared."

The waitress came up and they ordered coffee and sandwiches.

"What did you say?"

"I said it must be really upsetting that one of your closest friends just disappeared."

"Yeah, it … it was. You said the police would be releasing pictures of Elsie."

"It's to be expected. I'm surprised they haven't already done so. That may be because her parents are resisting that decision or …"

"Or?"

Chrissie's blue eyes were suddenly focused.

"Or they may think they are very close to a breakthrough."

Amy had the impression that Chrissie's skin had paled.

"What do you think, Amy?"

"What I think is interesting about this case is that she hasn't been found. Dead or alive. If she is dead nine times out of ten by this time her remains would be found. So I think Elsie's still alive and if she is alive I don't think she is alone hiding out in a motel someplace. I don't think she's alone at all. Somebody's protecting her. Moreover, why would she want to leave her parents and cause so much pain to everybody. So it's pretty big and deadly secret."

The waitress arrived with their coffees and sandwiches.

Amy watched the girl as she sipped her coffee. Then.

"I can see why you would think that."

"But it's not true?"

Chrissie was looking at her hands as she cut her sandwich.

"I don't know. It could be true. I mean it's a good theory, as far as it goes."

"And there would have to be a motive, a really good reason."

"That's true."

Now Chrissie's eyes were staring right into hers.

"But you don't know this reason?"

Chrissie sipped her coffee, took a bite of her sandwich. A sudden inspiration struck Amy.

"What about Janet? Do you think Janet knows about this … reason, this secret reason?"

Chrissie shook her head.

"No, Janet doesn't know. She may guess but she doesn't know."

"Which implies you know more than Janet, and Janet's your closest friend."

Chrissie nodded non-committally.

"Whatever."

Amy took a breath. Sipped her coffee. There was something impressive about this kid.

"So what do you know, Christine?"

The young girl didn't hesitate.

"Have you ever had a friend, Amy? Really had a friend?"

This time it was Amy who stared.

"What do you mean?" Though Amy knew exactly what Chrissie meant.

"Elsie's my friend. End of."

Amy watched the girl eat her sandwich. It was the end of the interview.

"OK."

Chapter 21

This was interesting. Chrissie had effectively told her that she knew a lot about Elsie's disappearance if not where she actually was. Of course, if the police or anybody else questioned her she would deny that she had said anything to Amy. So effectively again, she had taken Amy into her confidence. Chrissie was implying by her respecting of Elsie's trust in her that Elsie had good reasons for her disappearance. That afternoon she apprised Eddie of the new situation. Interesting said Eddie. Carry on.

She called Janet. Fixed an interview for the following noon. Same coffee house off Union Square. Amy went to bed that night thinking she was walking on egg shells.

When next day Janet walked into the room the whole café seemed to sigh. The girl was unspeakably beautiful. This time the microdress was lime green. Everybody in the room male and female, old and young wanted to fuck her. Amy's mouth was watering. Everybody in the room wanted to lift the hem of Janet's tiny dress and get to work on her cunt and asshole. Most people meet a woman like that once or twice in a lifetime. They are the ultimate currency of any age. What did the man say? Pricier than rubies.

Amy managed a smile.

"Coffee?"

"Just black."

"Anything to eat?"

"No, thank you."

Amy signaled the waitress.

"Two coffees please. Both black no sugar.

The girl shifted in her seat. It was extraordinarily erotic.

"Is there any news of Elsie, Amy?"

"De nada, as you might say."

Janet greeted this presumption with a thin smile.

"I too have heard nothing. It is worrying, no?"

"I spoke to Chrissie yesterday. We both think that Elsie is still alive."

Janet frowned delicately.

"Why do you think that, Amy?"

"Elsie has been missing for nearly a month. That's a long time for a missing person. Usually they are found – alive or dead within that time."

Amy was guessing but it seemed reasonable and it coincided with what she had learned in Sacramento during her PI training.

The girl arrived with their coffees. Janet digested this piece of information.

"So that is the good news?"

Amy wanted to say no, it is good news, what is the point of your expensive fucking private education if you can't get to use the fucking definite article correctly. However, she contented herself with.

"I wouldn't say it was good news. Let's just say it is not *bad* news."

"Si. I understand."

Amy wondered why she was getting so irritated by this beauty's complacent nonchalance. Try a different tack.

"So assuming Elsie's disappeared for her own reasons, can you imagine what those reasons might be? Janet sipped her coffee, even that trivial movement gave off an air of obscenity.

"Maybe she was afraid. Maybe somebody was threatening her and she was very frightened."

"What kind of somebody?"

She shrugged.

"Who can say? It is a dangerous world, no?"

"Is it, Janet? Is it a dangerous world?"

"Si, is dangerous. (You're fucking doing it again thought Amy.) In Texas Mehico is just across the river Rio Grande. The cartels run Mehico, run towns in United States too."

"You think the cartels are mixed up in Elsie's disappearance?"

That would be a new development thought Amy.

"Is possible. Anything is possible these days. These police I have been speaking to about Elsie, they have no imagination. They do not think how you say beyond the box."

"Outside the box."

"Yes, outside the box. They do not think outside the box. They are like the horses with those covers over their eyes."

"Blinkers. They have a blinkered view."

"Exactly, Amy. They are blinkered."

"Outside the cartels are there any other explanations you can think of?"

More obscene sipping of coffee.

"Maybe she is involved with a bad boyfriend. He has kidnapped her perhaps?"

"Any idea who this boyfriend might be?"

This time the smile was broad and confident.

"No idea!"

"How about Johnnie or Steve?"

"No, they are just boys. Innocent boys."

Not so innocent thought Amy.

75

"So are there any men involved?"

It was a straightforward question but the response was complicated. Her face remained impassive but Amy sensed her body tremor. Felt the faintest intimation of a kind of excitement or fear or … something.

"With Elsie, no, I don't think so."

"But I think you prefer men to boys. You said that once to me."

Once again that confident smile.

"Men are exciting, no? They know what they want. I find that exciting."

"What do men want, Janet?"

"They want to fuck you in the mouth, in the cunt, in the asshole. They do not care what you want. Just what they want!"

Amy was surprised to realize that she was shocked by this beautiful sixteen year old.

"Are you Catholic?"

"Of course."

"As a matter of fact so am I. Do you go to confession?"

Another broad smile.

"Of course. Every Sunday. So you are Catholic too?"

"Not a very good one."

"Not to worry. We are all sinners, no? But God forgives all!"

"I'm not sure about that."

"Si, he forgives everything. If you are contrite, penitent."

"And are you contrite, Janet?"

"Si, I am very contrite."

"So you let these guys fuck you everywhere. Maybe married guys but that is OK because on Sunday you are contrite?"

This time she laughed.

"It is good, no? Satisfaction guaranteed!"

"And are you seeing an older guy at the moment?"

The smile was still there.

"Not just one. They have friends, those friends have friends."

"So you admit that you're a slut?"

"Si, I was born to be. A real slut. I love it."

Amy stared at her. It was like looking in a mirror. To see yourself as you were at sixteen.

Amy nodded.

"Thanks, Janet. You have been really helpful."

Janet winked.

"De nada – as we say in Mehico!"

Chapter 22

"She's either a complete fantasist or she's a complete whore!"

Amy was sitting in her Pacific Heights apartment sipping a lot of Jack Daniel's and a little water. She was speaking to her boss on her Nokia.

"Well which?" said Eddie.

"Everything tells me No. 2. She has this extraordinary confidence. She's a sixteen year old who comes across like thirty five. She was wearing this microdress but barely uncrossed her legs. You know what that means! I think she loves to be a slut in fact she confessed as much. 'Si, I am slut, no?' These privately educated girls, they're unbelievable!"

Eddie thought of Jennifer and her English private education.

"It can push them to extremes. The important thing is does she know anything about Elsie's disappearance?"

"The funny thing is that I don't think she does which may mean that Chrissie is not confiding in her. They're best mates supposedly but her loyalty to Elsie over-rides her friendship with Janet. It's complicated."

"Did you indicate to Janet that Chrissie might know something?"

"Absolutely not. I think Chrissie trusts me up to a point and I want to keep it that way. Janet said that she had sex with adult men including married men. She's sex mad."

"Just like you … or me or April or whoever!"

"Nah, it's different with her. She's pretty cold and calculating. She's Catholic but she's a dealer – even with God. Like she's doing him favors. Like her contrition is so many greenbacks!"

"Interesting. You say that Chrissie probably knows where Elsie is but isn't saying out of loyalty?"

"Check."

"So why don't we follow Chrissie and see where she leads?"

"Because she's way too smart. She'd pick up on someone following her and I don't think an electronic tag would work, she could find it and that would be the end of her trusting me."

"You're taking on a lot of responsibility. The client is her parents. If anything happened to Elsie. I don't have to draw you a picture."

"No, you don't. Chrissie was worried when I told her it was likely that police would be releasing pictures of Elsie as a missing person."

"So she's shacked up somewhere and Chrissie is getting food and drink to her."

"That would be difficult for Chrissie. There's probably a third party."

"Any ideas who that might be? One of the boys? Her boyfriend Billy?"

Amy took a swig of Mr Daniel's fine liquor. Shook her head.

"No, it's not Billy. Maybe Johnny or maybe Steve for different reasons. But they'd be taking an incredible risk. Chrissie is doing it out of love, frankly. Any third party would have to have a similar motivation."

"But not the boyfriend – Billy?"

She sighed.

"OK, I'll look into it."

Chapter 23

"Billy, we have reason to believe that Elsie is alive and hiding some place. We still don't know why she left home. Would you know anything about that?"

They were sitting in a quiet corner of the coffee house that Amy used for her research. Billy looked subdued and strained. It looked like he hadn't shaved for a couple of days. When he spoke Amy had to strain to hear.

"This is so crazy. One moment everything is totally normal we're talking about Thomas Wolfe, *Look Homeward, Angel*, the next she's just gone. Like that book *Gone Girl* – you know it? – and you think am I like the husband in that book who didn't know his wife at all? I keep trying to think of things I missed at the time. It's driving me nuts."

"And is there anything that comes to your mind?"

"No, except …"

"Except?"

"I think now that there was a side of Elsie that I didn't know anything about."

"Another side. What kind of side?"

"Well, that's real difficult because she didn't really reveal it. Sometimes in the middle of a conversation

I would sense that her mind was elsewhere and a different look would appear on her face."

"What kind of look?"

"A kind of smile that wasn't actually a real smile."

"Mona Lisa?"

"No, quite different. A kind of secretive smile."

"What did you feel when you saw that smile or non-smile?"

"I don't know. Kinda worried maybe. Sometimes almost annoyed that she was keeping something from me. And sometimes …"

"Sometimes?"

"This is difficult. Sometimes almost frightened. I've never thought about it before. You must be a good investigator!"

He smiled. It was the first time she had seen him smile. A smile of relief?

"Going back to what I said at the beginning – do you have any idea where she might be hiding, if she were hiding?"

He looked at her straight in the eye.

"No idea, no idea at all. We only met in public places. I have no idea where she might be. She certainly hasn't contacted me nor have I seen her."

Amy believed him. He had one last thing to say,

"It's funny, you have the same name as the girl in the book, *Gone Girl*!"

Amy grinned.

"The resemblance ends there!"

Chapter 24

Andrea Lennox was driving her red T-bird fast down the Pacific Coast Highway. She had left her tweeds and pearls at home exchanging them for a slutty hot pink skirt suit with her tits pushed up by push up bra. She wore a lot of make up. Most people wouldn't have recognized the private girls school principal.

She needed it and she deserved it she rationalized. This year in particular there were just too many pretty, rich young sluts. Funnily enough she thought of that gorgeous young whore Janet Suarez and that dirty little bitch Elsie Cromwell. She changed down to fourth and let the Thunderbird drift over a hundred. She had insisted on checking out the little slut's iPhone, seen the two pricks pic and the delicious little ass, not to mention sucking some nameless boy's penis. God, her cunt had leaked when she had seen the pics and looked up to see that Cromwell smirk. What's it going to be she said coldly, your parents or my pussy? Elsie just smiled and knelt between her open legs. God, what a come the little bitch had given her. When she had finished she laughed with an anytime you want, miss!

Now the little cunt had disappeared. She put her hand between her legs and thought languorously of Elsie being raped by a couple of black studs or three before being satisfyingly strangled. She groaned with pleasure as she realized the car was doing more than a hundred and ten and she throttled back. Now was not the time to spoil it all by having a high speed crash.

She had made contact with the cartel who owned the house in Tijuana through her cocaine dealer, a nice Mexican boy.

She arrived at the large Spanish style house on time just before midnight. She took off the suit in a large ante room with the other women who ranged in age between twenty and sixty. Like the others she wore slutty underwear and stockings and high heels. They walked pretty much together into a large room with two log fires blazing and brilliantly lit by a dozen large chandeliers. There were perhaps fifty cartel gangsters there, generally heavily built, naked, tattooed with almost universally dark brown to black hostile and contemptuous eyes. The women arranged themselves in a circle looking at the men as they masturbated their cunts and nipples. The men held erect pricks and spat and swore at the sluts. And then suddenly the men surged forward and grabbed tits and ass. There were at least twice as many men as women and in a moment Andrea was lying astride one man on his back as another fucked her asshole. Some other man was pissing on her face.

The whole room was a roaring tumult as men and women cursed each other and groaned in countless orgasms. But it was only when Andrea Lennox was writhing covered with shit and piss and cum that she finally experienced release from the torment she daily experienced at the sight of all the teenage bitches she was notionally responsible for. She thought of Janet Suarez then and how she would crush her beautiful young body in the shit she was presently lying in. A nameless man was standing astride her prone body and masturbating over her shitty brown limbs.

"That's right, you bastard, spunk me good. Aaah, clever boy!"

God, she felt good!

Chapter 25

Elsie's photograph was on the front page of the Chronicle. Sixteen year old daughter of acclaimed San Francisco architects missing for a month. Elsie Cromwell mysteriously disappeared after Christmas sometime before her sixteenth birthday. We just want her back state her parents Alan and Susan Cromwell we are in no way blaming her, please just call etc, etc. There has been no ransom demand.

Susan Cromwell had phoned Eddie the previous evening warning him that they had spoken to the police about their decision to go public.

It was ten in the morning and they were all sitting in Eddie's office. Eddie was speaking.

"I'm sorry, Amy, but we have to follow Chrissie. OK, April?"

"I'll pick up on her from when she leaves school today."

Amy was fiddling with her hair distractedly.

"Amy?"

"I hate this, Eddie, she'll just go to ground, especially now it's all over the news. I heard it on the radio driving in."

"Now's the time. She'll want to talk to Elsie about what to do. We don't know if a third party is involved. It may be Janet ..."

"It's not Janet."

"How can you be so sure, Amy?"

"Trust me, April – it's not Janet."

"OK."

They were all tense. The only break they had had was Amy's assertion that Chrissie knew where Elsie was hiding out. It was the most delicate of situations. If they told the police which technically they should have done, the cops would have hauled her in with unpredictable consequences for Elsie. Girls of that age could be very stubborn and if Chrissie were unable to contact Elsie that very fact could trigger Elsie's Plan B. What was the Hippocratic oath? First do no harm.

Eddie took the girls out for a brunch at the usual café. There was not a lot of conversation. They were all focusing in their different ways on the new situation.

Chapter 26

April was following Chrissie's Honda over the golden
Gate Bridge. It was nine at night but things were made
easier by the fact that the little Honda's right rear light was
slightly damaged leaking yellow light. This allowed April
in her BMW to lie two or three cars behind. Somehow she
wasn't surprised when Chrissie took the Sausalito turn off.
Now there wasn't so much traffic and April cruised slowly
on side lights as Chrissie went along the harbor looking for
a parking space. Fifty yards behind, April cut her lights
and waited. Parked facing the water Chrissie was still
behind the wheel talking on her cell phone. A couple of
minutes later she got out and looked around. She was
wearing a hooded jacket with the hood covering her hair.
Dark jeans and sneakers. She began to walk back toward
the silent BMW. April was already lying along the front
seats. Shit. Chrissie walked by ten yards away. April
watched her using the mirror of her compact – an old trick.
She gave her twenty seconds and cautiously raised her
head. No Chrissie! April opened the car door with the
faintest of clicks and eased herself into the freezing air.
Then she saw the steps leading down to the quay where
numerous boats were berthed. She crept down the steps.

All the boats were dark and silent save for one which shed the faintest glimmer of light. April moved closer. She had to have a positive ID. She insinuated herself on to a neighboring boat and peered into the tiny illuminated porthole. Nothing. Then suddenly the profile of a young woman that April immediately recognized as Elsie.

April froze praying the face didn't turn to see her in the yellow light less than ten feet away. The profile still talking disappeared again. April crept off her boat and strode smoothly back to her BMW, lay on the front seats again and called Eddie on her Nokia.

"I've found her. She's in a boat moored to a quay in Sausalito. Should I approach?"

"Is she alone?"

"No, the subject is with her, talking, maybe others."

Eddie hesitated. They had no powers of arrest.

"Stay where you are. Are you in the Beemer?"

"Yes."

"I'm calling the cops."

"OK. I'm on the main quay. I'll flash my lights when I see the cop cars."

Which was all well and good except that five minutes later Chrissie and Elsie exited their boat and strode past April's BMW talking quietly. April called Eddie.

"They're moving, should I follow?"

"Yes, I'll call the cops!"

That was the moment when there was a sharp rap on April's window. She looked first at a small handgun and then Elsie's cold dark eyes. The automatic made a small circular motion. April turned on the ignition and pressed the window button. One cold word.

"Keys."

April pulled them out of the ignition and slowly, very slowly handed them into the small gloved hand.

"Don't fuck with us." It didn't sound like a privately educated voice. Then they were gone. She told Eddie to go to Pacific Heights pick up her spare set in her dressing table drawer and come over.

Chapter 27

The cops – SFPD and Sausalito sheriffs both – were
something less than sympathetic as they spoke first to
April stranded by her car, "Don't you carry spare keys,
miss" (April managed to restrain her "Ma'am, I think you
mean") and then Eddie frustrated at the time it had taken to
find said keys in various of April's dressing table drawers.
It was obvious from their attitude that female PIs in the
notoriously fey San Francisco were all too liable to
hallucination – that was when they weren't openly ogling
the lady's curves. The fact that there were four of them
only heightened their lasciviousness.

It was only when they checked with their databases and
found that the yacht in question belonged to one James
Middleton evident father to Chrissie that they reluctantly
quizzed April on what she had seen. Again, April
restrained herself from pointing out that she was the first
criminal investigator to have actually cast eyes on the
missing Elsie in over a month. As I say it was not a happy
meeting.

At five they called James Middleton on his cellphone and
asked him if his teenage daughter were at home. It took a
minute to discover that she wasn't. What was this about,

officer? If Mr Middleton could stay at his address officers would speak to him shortly. What was shortly? Shortly, sir and the cop ended the conversation.

Their last words to Eddie before they all drove off indicated that they would appreciate it if he and Miss van Buren could present themselves at SFPD central precinct downtown at say eleven this morning. Eddie, yawning now, agreed.

"One last thing, sir. (April gritted her teeth). This is now a criminal investigation. Your colleague was threatened with a small arms pistol whether real or fake."

"I understand," said Eddie.

When Eddie finally arrived back at North Beach and before throwing himself fully clothed into bed he telephoned Amy about this night's events.

"Told you," said a sleepy Amy. "That Chrissie is smart for her age."

Eddie could see further tension between the girls on its inevitable way.

"Get your glad rags on for ten. I'll pick you up with April, we have an appointment at SFPD central precinct at eleven. Make sure you have all relevant notes etc."

"See you at ten."

"Because Elsie pulled a gun on April it's now a criminal investigation. I'll speak to the Cromwells after we have seen the cops."

"Check," said Amy.

Chapter 28

Lieutenant Kamakura was trying to be patient.

"You say you had evidence that Middleton was in contact with Cromwell, was probably helping to prevent Cromwell's apprehension and protection by the authorities as a minor due the state's responsible care and yet you did not notify the SFPD of said evidence."

Eddie looked at Amy.

"Agent Fairfax?"

"We were hired by the Cromwells to find their daughter, Elsie. Following our investigations we entertained the suspicion that one or more of Elsie's friends were colluding with Elsie in hiding her. Chrissie Middleton in particular talked of her loyalty to Elsie and that such loyalty might outweigh any other considerations. When I tried to pursue her knowledge of Elsie's whereabouts she clammed up. We decided to follow her as that was in the remit of our responsibility to our client. Namely to find Elsie. Miss van Buren was delegated to surveil Chrissie as she was unknown to her. There was no criminal element at that stage. Simply a missing person."

Amy thought that was pretty good. However she was not sure that Kamakura was about to share her view.

"What in fact you and your colleagues did was to indicate by your actions that your abilities were superior to those agencies who had proper jurisdiction. You knew little or nothing of Elsie's circumstances and ended up provoking matters into a criminal situation."

"I don't regard your analysis as a fair or accurate one, " said Amy primly.

"You don't, huh? You should know from your recent training in Sacramento that where minors are involved you have a special responsibility to consider unpredictable and dangerous eventualities. You and your colleagues should have at least notified us of your proposed actions and afforded us the opportunity to take our own appropriate action. Am I not correct in my ... analysis?"

Amy was silent. Eddie interposed.

"Hindsight is a wonderful thing, lieutenant. We were very close to finding Elsie and escorting both girls back to their respective parental homes. Nothing in any of the young persons behaviors had indicated that any of them was in possession of firearms. Neither had the Cromwells or any other parent or guardian indicated that any of their children had access to weapons. These were respectable and responsible professional people with their respectable privately educated children. As soon as Agent van Buren had faced a drawn weapon she called the police. I would say that Jackson & Major carried out their investigations professionally."

For the first time Amy noticed the stenographer in the corner. Jackson & Major's reputation it seemed was on the line. Kamakura stared at Eddie.

"OK, Jackson ..."

"Mr Jackson."

"OK, Mr Jackson. I am notifying you officially that your actions are being investigated by the DA's office. You will be hearing from them. In the meantime, this is now a criminal investigation and any unwanted interference by you or your colleagues will be prosecuted and you will be consequently arraigned. Is that clear to you all?"

Discretion is the better part of valor. Eddie had read that somewhere.

"I will notify my clients that Elsie's disappearance is now a police matter."

They filed out of Kamakura's office. Asshole muttered April.

"They're blaming us for changing it into a criminal investigation. Kamakura's unbelievable!"

"Get used to it," said Eddie. "The cops are always right. In any case we now have to deal with the Cromwells and their gun toting daughter. No doubt we'll be hearing from the Middletons as well."

They went to their local diner for a much needed lunch.

Chapter 29

"I can't believe that Elsie had a gun! What kind of a gun for chrissakes?"

Susan Cromwell was furious. It was obvious she blamed Jackson & Major for this horrific turn of events. Her husband simmered alongside.

"It was dark but it looked like an old automatic, possibly a Beretta or an old Colt. I was pretty sure it was the real thing."

Eddie spoke quietly.

"What Agent van Buren means is that the gun wasn't a fake. Criminals often use fakes as sometimes they can get away with a misdemeanor. It's a common misapprehension."

"Are you saying that Elsie's a criminal? Susan was white with fury.

"I'm afraid Mrs Cromwell that threatening with a weapon is a serious felony in the state of California as it is anywhere in the United States – even in Texas!"

Eddie's attempt to lighten the mood only exacerbated the Cromwells' hostility.

"This is going nowhere," stated Alan, "we're wasting our time with these incompetents."

Amy had had enough.

"Has it not occurred to you that your daughter is in desperate straits? She left home for no reason that we have been able to discover, that her friend Chrissie has compromised herself as they are now both felons on the run, that any law enforcement agents will be justified in treating them as armed and dangerous. Are you people for real?"

Susan Cromwell recovered herself.

"This is completely unacceptable. We shall be lodging a complaint about your casual investigations and about this agent's insulting and ignorant behavior and attitude. You will not be receiving the balance of your fee."

The Cromwells stalked out.

April picked out a Lucky from the silver box and lit it. She spoke to nobody in particular.

"That wasn't so smart."

Amy was too angry to reply.

Eddie pulled out the office bottle of Jack Daniel's and poured them all three fingers.

"It's been a long night and a long day. We'll meet here tomorrow morning at ten and take it from there. Cheers."

They drank the whiskey and went their separate ways.

Chapter 30

The next morning James and May Middleton telephoned to say they would like to come in and discuss their daughter's situation. Jim Middleton was a well dressed business man in his late forties early fifties and his wife was a quiet smiling woman perhaps five years younger. Amy explained that she had had two or three conversations with Chrissie and that she had become increasingly convinced that Chrissie was supporting Elsie and perhaps knew where she was hiding. Her colleague April van Buren had followed her by car to the Middletons' yacht in Sausalito.

"We are extremely concerned for Chrissie. We had no idea that our boat was being used by Chrissie and Elsie. It is unused in the winter months. The harbormaster is supposed to check out all the boats as a matter of routine. He knows Chrissie and I guess if he had seen her on the boat with a friend he wouldn't have been too worried though I would have expected him to notify us that our child had been present."

"Have you spoken to him?"

"Not yet. I thought I would speak to you first."

"I guess you were aware of Elsie's disappearance. Did you have any idea as to why she had disappeared? Did you discuss it with Chrissie?"

May answered.

"Chrissie became quite impatient when I brought the subject up. She just said it was a complete swearword mystery. I guess we now know why she was so little forthcoming."

"We understand from the police that a handgun is involved?"

James Middleton's face was strained and pale. Amy spoke.

"Elsie pulled a gun and threatened my colleague Ms van Buren. Your daughter could be accused of being an accessory. We think you should know that the Cromwells are no longer our clients. The San Francisco police have jurisdiction in what is now a crime situation. If you have any thoughts or knowledge of your daughter's whereabouts you should notify them just as we are also bound to notify them if we have knowledge of Chrissie's or Elsie's location."

Eddie interposed.

"Normally, we respect client confidentiality but I daresay that you were aware that the Cromwells had hired us to attempt to find their daughter, Elsie …"

The Middletons nodded.

"Yeah, we knew that from Chrissie."

"The biggest mystery is why Elsie ran off in the first place. It is possible that Chrissie knows the reason but she appears to be ultra loyal to Elsie. If you are able to discover why the two girls ran off you must call the police."

The Middletons nodded again.

"Was there anything else?" asked Eddie.

Middleton shook his head.

"I guess not. We appreciate your talking to us Mr Jackson, Miss Fairfax.

"We earnestly hope that there is a happy outcome."

They all shook hands.

Chapter 31

That night Amy had a terrible nightmare. She and Chrissie were talking to each other on a moving train. Gradually the car began to fill with other passengers who moved in from adjoining cars. Quietly, they surrounded Amy and Chrissie and began to caress them. Suddenly, their mouths opened exposing long fangs and began to take bloody bites out of any exposed flesh.

Amy tried to scream but could not. Finally she managed a kind of growl and woke up. Her jaw was shaking. It took a while for it to stop shaking. She got out of bed, put on a robe and lit one of her Dunhills.

So much for professional detachment she thought. First the Underwoods and now this. Why had Elsie left home, why had Chrissie supported her to the extent of going on the run herself? What was eating the two girls, quickly rationalizing her dream. What did Elsie know?

The private investigator – any kind of detective – has a particular relationship with his or her imagination. Too little imagination and the detective may live in rude health but is useless as an investigator. Too much – and madness calls. The investigator is not dissimilar to the psychotherapist. The danger for the therapist is over identification with the client. What used to be called counter transference. F Scott Fitzgerald wrote arguably his greatest novel based on the phenomenon. The danger for the investigator is pretty much the same.

Amy had gotten close to Chrissie without being properly aware of it. She had recognized her own sixteen year old self discovering the power and excitement of sex, the fact of having something that was infinitely desirable to adult men – and women. Yes, she had seen herself in Chrissie – in some ways it was a pleasant recognition. What she hadn't seen was Elsie and what had happened to Elsie and more importantly what Elsie was prepared to do about it. Whatever "it" was.

It was not that she knew nothing about Elsie; she had spoken to the extraordinary Janet Suarez, had spoken to Billy Martinez each in their own ways both knowing and ignorant of the enigmatic Elsie, the Elsie who had waved her handgun with such casual effrontery in front of April's nose; and Amy had confronted the Cromwells' rage and arrogance. Elsie captivated people like Janet captivated people except the captivation was different, very different.

No, Amy had stumbled into a nightmare but what the nightmare was really about – well, that was another matter!

Chapter 32

On Friday night Eddie hired a hotel room on Geary and three whores. Eddie specified that the whores were to be aged between twenty and thirty and dressed in tight black business skirt suits. He, April and Amy were drinking Jack D in their underwear when the girls arrived. Eddie knew that Amy was close to breaking point. But even he was surprised at her strength and violence. As soon as the girls had been paid Amy seized one of the two dark hared whores by the throat and smashed her against a wall. She then reached under her skirt, forcing her hand between her thighs and into her cunt, ignoring the girl's protests. The four of them watched – Eddie fingering April's anus as Amy punched, kicked and fisted the struggling girl.

"Fuck you bitch!" And then started to bite the girl's breasts as she fisted her cunt. Eddie continued to finger April's asshole as April began to lick the blonde whore's cunt and asshole as she lay on the bed, skirt rucked around her waist, legs open and knees over her tits. The other black haired whore was sucking Eddie's dick. They all craned their necks to see what Amy was doing to dark haired whore number one.

Amy was going mad, she knew she wanted to kill this slut as she had killed – with others – a girl in London, England all those years ago. She began to deliberately strangle the bitch. The girl was young and strong but Amy was a trained martial artist. Amy orgasmed as she felt the girl's legs thrashing beneath her own body. Amy spat on the whore's contorted face and the moment passed. She released her grip and the girl gasped.

"Now eat me, cunt!" And sat on the girl's face. Eddie threw his black haired whore on the bed alongside April and the blonde, turned her over, lifted her buttocks and buggered the bitch as April fisted blondie's cunt.

They all began to relax and settle into a cycle of satisfying brutal fucking. The whores regained their confidence and began to grunt and swear in satisfaction whether real or contrived. Eddie looked over and saw Amy apparently swooning in pleasure as her bitch sucked her off, fingers in Amy's anus. April was pissing and shitting on her girl's face and breasts careless of sheets and clothes. Eddie did the same on his slut.

After a couple of hours, they showered, washed the bed linen as best they could and paid the three girls extra for their tolerant attitudes. When they had gone, Eddie spoke to his colleagues.

"Better?"

Amy smiled.

"God, yes."

"April?"

"Always."

Eddie kissed both the women tenderly.

"It'll be fine."

Chapter 33

And then nothing. And more nothing. Technically – since it had been witnessed – the Cromwells had terminated their contract though nothing had been put in writing. Chrissie and Elsie had disappeared. The city and state police had put out an APB covering all California. There had been further articles in the Chronicle, the Los Angeles papers and the usual TV companies like CNN. Daughter of famous San Francisco architects pulls handgun on cops was the slightly inaccurate headline. Jackson & Major kept their head down. The last thing that Eddie wanted was to be identified with the "cops".

The Middletons called occasionally desperately seeking news, any news of Chrissie. Nothing from the Cromwells. Janet Suarez uncharacteristically anxious spoke to Amy – she was so worried, had Amy heard anything. Amy explained that if she had she would have been obligated to inform the police. Conversely, said Amy, did Janet have any idea as to where the two girls *might* have gone? No, Amy, no idea. I am so worried.

Nothing from Steve or Johnnie. When Amy called them she got voicemail. They didn't call back. Everybody went to ground. Technically – again – Amy shouldn't have been calling them, the two boys, as the Elsie Cromwell case was closed but Eddie had allowed a certain leeway, given nothing was in writing except the original contract. Nothing from the school principal Andrea Lennox. Amy wondered about her. Kamakura called a couple of times just to chat really it seemed. Perhaps he was seeking some kind of enlightenment regarding teenage girls or maybe he was just on a fishing expedition.

It went on like that for a couple of weeks. There had been a lot of publicity, the girls' pictures pretty much everywhere, it seemed highly unlikely they were holed up in some motel. How about Vegas April asserted and they called Kamakura. Sixteen year old girls showing their IDs in Vegas would have sprung any number of red flags. Anyway it's covered.

No, they had to have a bolt hole someplace. California was huge, a lot of it effective wilderness. If they were prepared to rough it, they could be practically anywhere.

Amy and April talked about the missing girls. These kids were tough and resourceful they had begun to understand. Elsie in particular seemed to have hidden depths. Everybody who had known her had remarked on this mysterious watchful look she had occasionally revealed, however fleetingly. It was like a throwback to the Old

West, the Hole in the Wall gang, Butch Cassidy and SunDance. These girls had that coldness of glance, that survival instinct, that legacy of times when the only protection you had was your assessment of enigmatic situations and people and the speed and determination of your reactions. That American resourcefulness had been blurred in recent years with the modern obsession with "woke" with fairness and decency. But Americans were not English Amy had reflected, they had never been able to afford that kind of English tolerance or optimism.

No, Amy had begun to recognize the differences and Elsie and Chrissie were very much a case in point.

The revelation of these truths when it came was sudden and brutal.

Chapter 34

The noise in the small gymnasium was deafening. Bamboo staves clashed against each other or occasionally connected with *men* (helmet) or *do* (breastplate) all associated with *kiai* (shouts) as twenty men and a few woman practised *kendo* the art of swordmanship. They were all universally dressed in indigo jackets and *hakama*, long divided skirts – traditional Japanese clothing.

Eddie was fencing with Kamakura. They were of equal rank, *sandan* or third dan and of similar ability, the speed and agility of the younger was balanced against the experience and timing of the older man – or that was how Eddie rationalized it. For Eddie it was profoundly calming despite the noise and apparent aggression, a kind of active meditation. Eddie managed a good *do* cut, his specialty and both men bowed to each other as the session was called to an end by the dojo master.

After they had showered and stashed their *gi* and armor away they all retired to a neighboring bar where they drank pints of beer.

For Kamakura and Eddie it was always an interesting time. As *kendoka* they could enjoy a trust that to a degree transcended their roles of police lieutenant and private investigator. After the general group celebration of the delights of kendo the two men managed to find a quiet corner. Kamakura opened with:

"Anything new on the Cromwell case?"

Eddie shook his head.

"Nothing. The girls have been checking out some of their friends. They all claim to know nothing. The Middletons are super anxious. I would say they know nothing and they knew nothing about the girls using their yacht."

"What about the Cromwells?"

"Incommunicado. They blame us for provoking Elsie into using a you know what."

Kamakura nodded and sipped his beer.

"There's something about the Cromwells."

Kamakura's face was impassive but Eddie knew when his friend was holding something back.

"Yeah, what?"

Kamakura shifted in his seat. He was wearing a gray sweater and old blue jeans and old white sneakers. But Eddie knew his police Glock was always on him, probably in his armor bag.

"It's privileged information. Nothing in the public domain. The DA let it go."

Silence. Eddie knew better than to press the younger man.

"They received an official warning from us. They took a PC in for repair, the repair guy contacted us. They had been downloading obscene material."

"Both of them?"

"Yeah."

"What kind of stuff?"

Kamakura looked around. He grunted.

"The usual, violent rape etc."

"Paedo?"

"Not as such, the girls were young. Borderline."

"What was the Cromwells' attitude?"

"Pleaded ignorance, the internet is a free dimension, everybody is using this stuff. It was all just acting, the usual."

"Was the stuff just acting?"

Kamakura shook his head.

"We know this stuff. It's made by the cartels or East European and Russian gangs. No, it wasn't acting."

"How often do you give these warnings, cautions they call them in the UK I understand from Amy."

Kamakura took another swallow of beer.

"Not that often. The Cromwells seem to have powerful lawyer friends, they connected with the DA's office."

That might explain the Cromwells' aggression to Jackson & Major.

"So it was just bad luck that the Cromwells were found out, a repairman with scruples."

"Maybe a repairman with daughters."

Eddie nodded.

"The modern world, huh?"

Kamakura finished his beer.

"Tell me about it."

A woman sitting with a group of guys called out.

"Hey, what are you two sweet talking about?"

Eddie got up.

"Thanks, Bill. You got a nice *men* cut on me by the way!"

Kamakura grinned.

"I know!"

Eddie fitted his *shinai* case through the loops of his bag and walked out of the bar. If asked he always replied.

"Fishing."

Chapter 35

And then all hell broke loose. It started at 11am when Amy sitting in the office sipping a cup of coffee with Eddie received a call on her cell from an almost incoherent Chrissie.

"Elsie sent me out to the supermart on Divisadero to get more coffee and bread. When I left Janet was fine, they were both fine, just talking, you know, everything was just fine, and now ... oh god ..."

Chrissie was screaming. Amy spoke urgently, waving at Eddie.

"Calm down, Chrissie. First where are you?"

More screaming. Eddie was on his feet. What?

"Chrissie calm down. Where are you?"

"Elsie's gone. Janet's dead. She's been ... stabbed. Many times ... all over. Oh god, there's blood everywhere ..."

"Chrissie, I'm coming. Where are you?"

"A motel, off Divi. The Orchard, yes, The Orchard."

"Chrissie. This is very important. Do not touch anything. Do you understand. Say now you understand."

"I understand, Amy, I mustn't touch anything. Are you coming?"

"Yes, Eddie and I are coming. What room number at The Orchard?"

"Number three. I'll wait outside, OK?"

"We're leaving now. We'll be with you in ten, twenty minutes maximum. Stay outside."

She ended the call. She spoke to Eddie.

"We're driving now. I'll explain as we go. It's Chrissie calling from a motel The Orchard just off Divisadero. Janet's been stabbed. Elsie's gone. Come on."

Chrissie was sitting on the steps of Apt 3, smoking a cigarette with a shaking hand and white faced. A middle aged female was trying to talk to her. Eddie took over.

"Amy stay with her. Thank you ma'am, we'll take it from here. This is a probable crime scene. Edward Jackson, licensed private investigator."

Eddie entered the motel room. Janet was sprawled in an armchair. There were at least six entry wounds. A knife with a wooden handle was lodged between her breasts. Eddie touched an arm. The body was warm. She had died within the hour. He called Kamakura.

"Bill. The Cromwell case. Elsie's friend Janet Suarez …"

"I know Suarez."

"Suarez is dead, stabbed several times. I'm at a motel The Orchard, just off Divi, know it?"

"Any witnesses?"

"Chrissie Middleton. She's with us having notified us."

"Don't touch anything. We're on our way."
Eddie joined Amy and Chrissie outside. He spoke urgently to Chrissie.

"The police are coming. We've got maybe five minutes. Tell me everything you know. Now."
Chrissie was wide eyed.

"Elsie left home because she had seen her mom and pa fucking Janet. She didn't know whether her parents or Janet had seen her. She just left quietly and came to me. She said she would never go back home. I hid her on our boat."

"Where did Elsie get the gun?"

"I don't know. I don't know why she wanted to see Janet. I don't think Janet knew that Elsie had seen her with her parents. This is so crazy."
Eddie could hear the police sirens now.

"Were you aware that Elsie intended to kill Janet? This is very important."

"No, absolutely not. They were just talking and smiling when Elsie asked me to get the stuff from the shops, coffee and bread."

"Do you know where Elsie is now?"

Chrissie shook her head.

"I've no idea. Oh god, the cops are here."

The first black and white squealed to a stop a few feet from them. Two uniformed officers came out.

"Which of you is Eddie Jackson?"

"That would be me, officer and this is my colleague Amy Fairfax both attending the incident."

"And who are you, miss?"

"Chrissie Middleton. I called Amy and Mr Jackson came as well."

Kamakura's green Chrysler parked alongside the black and white. The uniformed cop touched his hat.

"Lieutenant."

"Jack you stay with these people. They're all provisionally under arrest. Ian, we're going in."

Within a minute other cars had arrived, Eddie recognized some of the CSI people. It was out of his hands now.

Chapter 36

The usual madness. Headlines all over the San Francisco Chronicle and the Texas papers – "Texas beauty multiple stabbed in San Fran horror" etc etc. The press outside Eddie's Post Street office were three and four deep with TV cameras and microphones sprouting throughout. Jackson & Major International were in the thick of it. Eddie made one statement basically saying he couldn't comment and referred them to the police amid universal groans.

Following Chrissie's statement to the police alleging the Cromwells' criminal involvement in and providing a pretext for their daughter's disappearance, a daughter who was the major suspect in a brutal killing everybody lawyered up. Statement from Cromwells' lawyer – our clients have nothing to say at this time in response to reported comments of a minor who is evidently in shock following a traumatic experience. Statement from the Suarez lawyer – our clients are having to come to terms with the tragic and brutal death of their daughter Janet. They have nothing to say at this time. They would be grateful if they could be allowed to grieve for their daughter. Statement from Middletons' lawyers – "our daughter who is only just sixteen has suffered the most terrible and traumatic experience. We have nothing to say at this time."

The police found the coffee – Guatemalan – and bread – rye – still in a brown paper bag on a shelf in the motel. Further investigation found the cashier at the checkout of a neighboring store that confirmed the check in the bag and the identity of the young girl who had paid for them with her debit card twenty minutes before her call to Amy.

Nevertheless, in the presence of a social worker and the Middletons' lawyers they grilled Chrissie for two hours, had a break for a coffee and sandwich and grilled her for another two hours. When did Elsie make her statements regarding Janet Suarez and her parents? Did Chrissie realize a crime had been committed if the alleged statements were true? Why did she not speak to her parents or … Ms Lennox? Was she being intimidated with a weapon by Elsie?

Chrissie replied to these questions stubbornly and consistently with – she's my friend and no, Elsie never threatened her. When the questioning became too demanding the social worker shook her head almost imperceptibly. Her lawyer on a couple of occasions interjected with – I think Chrissie has answered that question. When toward the end the policewoman asked Chrissie if she had witnessed the murder Chrissie collapsed in tears. No, I was buying the things at the store, don't you understand. The social worker snapped – Enough. After lengthy discussions with the DA's office no charges were preferred. She was returned to the arms of her weeping parents.

Kamakura handled the Cromwells. They flatly denied the allegations of statutory rape. (A) it was hearsay and (B) it came from a hysterical minor who perhaps had her own reasons for getting at her erstwhile friend's parents. Finally where was their daughter was it not possible that she had been kidnapped by Janet's killer?

"You were investigated a while back for accessing obscene material on your PC."

"Nothing was proven," snapped Susan, "and in any case everybody watches porn at some time!" For chrissakes she added for good measure.

"There is an APB out on your daughter who is the principal suspect in a vicious murder."

"Vicious is a prejudicial term, Lieutenant," murmured their lawyer.

"How would you describe a knife attack involving eight entry wounds?" asked Kamakura in his impassive fashion.

"Uncontrolled?" Never argue with a lawyer. Kamakura finished with

"Don't leave town. This interview is terminated for the present but we may have to speak to you again. About Elsie's access to a pistol."

"Can we go?" Susan was already on her feet, her husband white faced and rising shakily.

"You can go."

After they had vacated the interview room with their inevitable lawyer a young detective asked.

"What do you think, Lieutenant?"

Kamakura just grunted.

"Fuckers."

Chapter 37

The next few weeks were quiet. Eddie and April were busy on another insurance scam. Eddie finally agreed to approach Kirsty with a view to her starting training as a prospective PI. Only Amy was kicking her heels.

However, she felt calm. The Cromwell case had turned out to be her case. The fact that nobody had been arraigned for Janet's murder did not trouble her. Everybody knew that Elsie had killed her. Except the real criminals were her parents, respectable San Francisco architects whose daughter had destroyed any evidence of their crime. Nobody seemed to talk about that. It was not clear that the Suarez family knew of Chrissie's accusations regarding the Cromwells. Since it was all hearsay on Chrissie's part the Cromwells had probably obtained an injunction to prevent Chrissie repeating what Elsie had told her about Janet and her parents.

Ironic that it had started out as a missing person case. Elsie was really missing now. Whether her parents were secretly in touch with her was a mystery. The FBI would be monitoring the Cromwells' telephone calls, texts and emails but there were plenty of other forms of communication on social media.

Chrissie and Amy managed to meet up for a coffee at a nondescript place south of Market.

She looked older and thinner. She wore a Covid mask which didn't attract attention, people still wore them. Amy asked her.

"How are you?"

Chrissie spoke quietly, Amy had to strain to hear her.

"OK, I guess. I'm back at school. The other girls have been very decent about things. Nobody talks about Elsie or Janet. Miss Lennox spoke to the whole school. Great tragedy, blah, blah but we have to all go on and support each other. Actually, she was OK. Said her door was always open.

"My folks have been great. I'm real lucky. The police said that I'm to have no contact with the Cromwells or Suarezes which is a big relief. I don't see the boys, Steve or Johnnie anymore. I'm pretty happy about that. They were really Janet's and Elsie's friends."

She was silent for a long half minute.

"I can't believe that Janet's dead. Have you heard from Elsie?"

Amy now realized why Chrissie had wanted to speak with her. She shook her head.

"There's been no contact. A couple of reports of sightings. One from Cape Town, South Africa. Another from Singapore. It's probably bullshit. You always get these false sightings."

"Elsie always had money. I don't know how she got it. Her parents I suppose. She ... she always had this mysterious side. It was part of her ... charm. I now realize that I didn't really know her at all. Kind of scary."

Amy reach out and touched her arm.

"Don't blame yourself. I think Elsie was a mystery to a lot of people and when you're fifteen, sixteen it doesn't really show. Girls especially at your age are evolving, changing. I think a couple of teachers maybe felt something."

Chrissie nodded. She didn't ask the name of the teachers.

"How are your studies?"

"Good. I'm getting interested in psychology. It's a cool subject. People are real interesting!"

Amy smiled.

"Well, you've had plenty of psychology over the last while!"

Chrissie grinned. It was the first time Amy had seen her smile for a long time.

"Sure have! Amy?"

"Yes?"

"I don't want this to be the end. I'd like us to be friends. You're one of the few people I've been able to trust since ... you know."

Amy felt the tears in her eyes. She took the girl's hand.

"Of course, darling. Of course we're friends. Anytime you want just call me!"

As she walked back to Post Street, Amy realized that finally she had achieved something, that she was a bona fide investigator. That she was the real McCoy.

Coda

Halfway through April on a clear spring day Eddie's phone rang.

"Eddie Jackson speaking."

"Hi. It's Elsie Cromwell."

Eddie waved frantically to April and Amy. They were sitting at their desks.

"I'm putting you on speaker phone, Elsie."

"Sure."

Her voice, calm not unpleasant filled the room. Eddie pushed the record button on his desk recorder.

"We get a lot of fake calls, Elsie," lied Eddie, "Can you identify yourself?"

"My name is Elspeth Mary Cromwell. I was born on October 23rd 2006 in Mill Valley. You have a naturalized English agent Amy Fairfax who was born and grew up in Liverpool, England and went to a convent school there. She is of course a Catholic. She met with Chrissie in the Franklin a coffee house off Union Square. How am I doing?"

"That's fine, Elsie. What can I do for you?"

"You can tell everybody who's interested that I am fine. You'll be able to trace this call to the Colombian

Ecuador border. I've gotten a good job under a different name obvs and I'm making friends. I will not be coming back to the States and I'm not sorry about anything. Other people should be sorry."

"When you say other people do you mean your parents? Chrissie said a few things about your folks."

"Let's just say they killed Janet. Not literally maybe, but they killed her."

"Did you stab Janet?"

"Nice try, Mr Jackson but I'm not here to make any confessions. I'm here to tell you that things have panned out like I expected. I'm not what you might call a good person, but I've got high hopes, high apple pie in the sky hopes. Is Amy there?"

"I'm here, Elsie."

"You did well, Amy. Maybe we'll meet up some day if you're down Mexico way."

"I'd like that."

"Good, you've got style, sweetheart!"

A silence.

"That's all folks."

The phone went dead. They all looked at each other. They spoke collectively.

"Wow!"

Eddie called Kamakura.

"Just heard from Elsie Cromwell. Says she's in Colombia Ecuador. I recorded the conversation."

"Get your asses over here."

Printed in Great Britain
by Amazon